Walt Disney's
MICKEY MOUSE
and the
Great Lot Plot

GOLDEN PRESS
Western Publishing Company, Inc.
Racine, Wisconsin

Fifth Printing, 1978

"Look at that!" Morty and Ferdie dropped their bat and ball and stared at the sign in front of them. THIS LAND FOR SALE!

"I can't believe it!" said Minnie Mouse. "This is the only vacant lot left for blocks around."

"Maybe whoever buys the land will let children play here," Mickey Mouse said hopefully.

"I'm going to buy it," said a voice behind them. It was Uncle Scrooge McDuck. "It's right next to my money bin, and it's the best place for my new business—SCROOGE'S PERFECTLY PLANTED, PICKED AND PROCESSED, PATENTED PICKLED PRESERVES!"

Morty and Ferdie wrinkled their noses. "Ugh! How can anyone think pickled preserves are more important than baseball?"

But Scrooge was very sure they were. "SCROOGE'S PERFECTLY PLANTED, PICKED AND PROCESSED, PATENTED PICKLED PRESERVES will be a good business," he said. Then he turned and walked away to his money bin.

Mickey and the others followed. They found him seated on a big pile of money, wiggling his toes and smiling happily.

"Won't you please think it over, Uncle Scrooge?" Mickey asked. "The children really need a place to run and play."

"No!" answered Uncle Scrooge. "My mind is made up, and that's final!"

"But playgrounds are important!" insisted Mickey.
Then, before he quite knew what he was saying, he
had made an announcement of his own. "*I'm* going
to buy the lot, and I'll make it into a playground for
everyone to enjoy."

Scrooge laughed so hard he rolled off the pile of
money. "Where will *you* get the money to buy this
lot?" he demanded.

As they left the money bin, Mickey's brave smile
changed to a frown. "Where *will* I get the money?"
he wondered.

But Minnie and the boys were bubbling with ex-
citement. "Why, we'll earn it!" they exclaimed.
"Don't worry, Mickey. Our friends will be happy to
help, too!"

And so they were! Those next few weeks, Mickey's friends were the busiest people in town. Busiest of all was Mickey himself.

He helped Donald Duck and his nephews wash cars. (Then he helped dry Huey, Dewey, and Louie, who got as wet as the cars they were washing.)

He helped Goofy, whose dog-walking job became too much for him to handle alone.

He helped Morty and Ferdie sell the pies and cakes that Minnie and Daisy Duck baked.

At the end of the month, Mickey counted up all the money that everyone had earned and given to him. It came to exactly five hundred dollars. That wasn't much, and Mickey was worried!

The next day he went to see Uncle Scrooge. "I'm very sad," he said. "All together, we've only been able to earn five hundred dollars, Uncle Scrooge, and I know that isn't enough money to buy the lot. *You* certainly can pay much more than that for it."

"Too bad, Mickey," Uncle Scrooge said, smiling. "Looks like the lot will be mine. It's sure a perfect place for my new pickled preserve factory."

Later that day, Scrooge walked happily down the street and stopped in front of the empty lot.

"Hi, Uncle Scrooge." There were Morty and Ferdie. "Got any jobs you want done?"

"Certainly not!" snapped Uncle Scrooge. "The only help I need is in understanding what's so important about a playground. A lot of foolishness, if you ask me. Humph!"

"We can't tell you—" said Morty.

"But we can show you," added Ferdie.

"Here, catch!" Morty shouted.

And before he knew it, Uncle Scrooge was out on the empty lot, playing a fast game of baseball.

It was nearly dark when the three finally sat
down to rest.

"Well, Uncle Scrooge," said Morty, "now do you
see what's so great about a playground?"

Uncle Scrooge was puffing so hard he couldn't
answer them.

The next day, the boys were waiting when Uncle
Scrooge came down the street.

"Tag!" shouted Morty.

"You're it!" yelled Ferdie.

And before he knew what had happened, Uncle
Scrooge was chasing the boys across the field.

"You can play all kinds of good games on a playground," said Morty when they stopped to rest at last.

"Humph!" Uncle Scrooge humphed. This time he was so tired that he fell asleep right there under a tree, and while he slept, he had a very strange dream. It was like no dream Uncle Scrooge had ever had before.

The next day, Mickey and his friends watched as the owner of the land put up a new sign on the lot. It said: SOLD TO SCROOGE McDUCK.

Everyone groaned—everyone, that is, except Scrooge. He was overjoyed.

As they all turned to leave, their faces sad, Scrooge shouted, "Wait here a few minutes. I have a surprise for you all!"

Soon workmen began to arrive. They lifted swings and slides into place! They started to dig a swimming pool! In the corner, they marked the lines for a baseball diamond!

Scrooge just stood there and grinned, while Mickey
and his friends gave three tremendous cheers.

"Uncle Scrooge," Mickey asked, "how can we ever
thank you enough? We're awfully glad you changed
your mind! Now we can buy *uniforms* for all of the
baseball team using our five hundred dollars!"

The day of the first game in the new park finally

arrived. Uncle Scrooge was given the honor of hitting the very first pitched ball.

"Hurrah!" the crowd cheered as the ball soared into the air.

The cheer was cut short by the tinkling of glass. The ball had crashed through a window in Scrooge's own money bin!

"Oh, oh! Sorry about your window, Uncle Scrooge,"
called Mickey.

But Uncle Scrooge was already on his way to first
base. "It's only glass," he shouted over his shoulder.
"But did you see that? I do believe I hit a home run!"

The Happiest, Most Heartwarming Publishing Event Of Our Time

Relive with your child the hours of joy Little Golden Books once brought you...

58 ALL-TIME CLASSICS

Little Golden Books
IN PERMANENT LIBRARY FORM
14-DAY FREE TRIAL OFFER!

The Little Golden Book Library

4 HANDSOME VOLUMES

- 384 pages in each volume . . . more than 1500 in all
- More than 1000 full-color Illustrations—a collector's gallery by some of the most distinguished children's artists of our time
- Bindings as strong as they are handsome—made to last for years
- A sturdy, decorative slipcase to keep this precious possession safe from harm

OUR WONDERFUL WORLD

FAIRYTALES AND RHYMES

BEDTIME STORIES

GOLDEN FAVORITES

The Little Golden Book Library

The little elephant danced along leaving wreckage behind him, until one day, he met a parrot. "Why are you shaking the jungle all to pieces?" cried the parrot, who had never before seen an elephant. "What kind of animal are you, anyway?"

REMEMBER how you listened spellbound as your parents read you these magical tales: Remember your pride when you were able to read them for yourself? Now you can relive those golden hours and share your joy with your child. THE LITTLE GOLDEN LIBRARY is an invitation to reading no child can resist. Stories just for fun . . . fantasy . . . beloved fairy tales . . . perky nursery rhymes . . . fascinating facts

58 ALL-TIME CLASSICS

GOLDEN FAVORITES

The Poky Little Puppy • Tootle • The Tawny Scrawny Lion • Scuffy the Tugboat • The Saggy Baggy Elephant • and 9 more all-time favorites

OUR WONDERFUL WORLD

My First Golden Geography • Wonders of Nature • About the Seashore • Baby Farm Animals • Dogs, Cats • Our Flag • and nine more magical introductions to the great world around us

BEDTIME STORIES

The Golden Sleepy Book • The Kitten Who Thought He Was a Mouse • The New Baby • What If? • Hush, Hush, It's Sleepytime • and seven more happy tales to dream on

FAIRY TALES AND RHYMES

The Little Golden Mother Goose • Jack and the Beanstalk • Three Little Kittens • Puss in Boots • Thumbelina • and ten more of the tales that live forever in your heart

Available By Mail Order Only — Return Your Reservation Certificate Today!

14-DAY FREE TRIAL RESERVATION CERTIFICATE

The world's best-loved books – for the world's best-loved children

The Little Golden Book Library TL2

YES-Please send me THE LITTLE GOLDEN BOOK LIBRARY for free 14-day examination. I understand I can return the four volumes to you without obligation within 14 days if I am not delighted with them. If I decide to keep them, you will bill me at the low price of just $5.95, and then $6.00 a month for two months (a total of only $17.95). A small charge will be added to my first invoice for postage, handling, and local sales tax.

Name_____

Address_____

City_____ State_____ Zip_____

Signature_____

(Please sign here. If under 21, have parent or guardian sign)

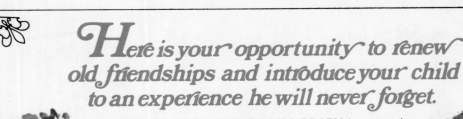